This book belongs to

....

Copyright © 2013

make believe ideas ltd

The Wilderness, Berkhamsted, Hertfordshire, HP4 2AZ.

www.makebelieveideas.com

Written by Tim Bugbird.
Illustrated by Stuart Lynch.
Designed by Annie Simpson and Sarah Vince.

Paulette the pinkest puppy in the world

Tim Bugbird · Stuart Lynch

make
believe
ideas

This is the tale of a puppy –
a puppy whose name was Paulette.
She was much like her brothers and sisters,
with a difference you'd never forget.

She had blue eyes like her sister, Bessy,
and big ears like her brother, Dale,
and just like her cousin, Jessy,
the cutest curly tail.

But one quite remarkable feature
meant Paulette was never in sync.
A truly unusual creature . . .

Paulette was totally PINK!

Not **gold**,

not **brown**,

not **black**,

or **white**,

not **green**,

or **red**,

or **blue**,

or **purple**,

or **yellow**
(with dots and **stripes**),

Paulette was **too pink** to be true!

This would have been **fine** and *dandy*

for a **piglet**,

a **starfish**

or **bird**.

But a **puppy**
the colour of **candy?**
The idea was simply
absurd!

Wherever she went, puppies would point and say,

"Well, look at that!

Paulette looks silly.
I mean to say,
really?"

So she tried
to hide under
a hat!

But the trouble with wearing a **big**, floppy hat,
while it covered up
some of the **pink**,

was she'd bump into things with a
BANG and a SPLAT!
It drove Paulette to the brink!

And then, one day, she had a knock –
it was **truly** the **final straw** –
she tripped on a **trike**,
which gave her a **shock**

and she fell, with a CRASH,
to the floor!

She knocked herself out but soon came around
and she grabbed what she thought was a post.
But the post was a ladder, not stuck in the ground.
"Uh-oh!" she thought, "I'm toast!"

As the ladder wobbled, it knocked a pail
of paint that was high on a sill.
The puppies below began to wail,
"Look out! It's going to spill!"

The petrified pups simply **froze** –
they didn't have time
to **think.**

Covered in **gunk** from their **heads** to their **toes** — their **coats** were **sticky** and **pink!**

The gloop wouldn't wash out
and nor would the goo,
so Paulette's mum
took out her clippers.
There was only one thing
she could possibly do,
but it gave the poor pups
the shivers!

Paulette's mum clipped each one –
it felt like such a shame.

But the puppies saw,
when the job was done,
underneath they were all the same!

"You're not so **different** after all,"
said Mum to Paulette, with a **wink.**

"And when they look back,
I think they'll recall
it was **nice** to be a bit **pink!**"

It could have been a **disastrous** day had Paulette not been the sort to look at things a **different** way. From the **fuss** sprung a **fabulous** thought!

She opened a salon –

Pink Cutz and More –

giving pedicures, perms and dip-dyes.

She was the **bark** of the park,

now everyone saw

Paulette through a fresh pair of eyes.

Pink Cutz & More!

Her clientele were the smartest in town,
with coats combed, braided and curled.

And Paulette became famous for miles around . . .

for being the **happiest pup** in the **world!**